Wilma Mankiller

Wilma Mankiller

Caroline Lazo

Peacemakers

DILLON PRESS
New York

Maxwell Macmillan Canada
Toronto

Maxwell Macmillan International
New York   Oxford   Singapore   Sydney

To the children of the Cherokee Nation

The author and publisher would like to give special thanks to Wilma Mankiller for her help and kindness in assisting with this project.

Photo Credits

Cover: The Cherokee Nation.
Jim Argo: 12. The Bettman Archive: 45. Gwendolyn Cates: 2, 31, 50, 57, 60. Gamma Liaison: 42. Tom Gilbert: 46. Lawrence Migdale: 38. The Cherokee Nation: 8, 17, 20, 27, 34, 40, 53. Sygma: 10.

Book design by Carol Matsuyama

Library of Congress Cataloging-in-Publication Data

Lazo, Caroline Evensen.
   Wilma Mankiller / by Caroline Lazo. — 1st ed.
     p. cm. — (Peacemakers)
   Includes bibliographical references and index.
   ISBN 0-87518-635-1
   1. Mankiller, Wilma Pearl, 1945- —Juvenile literature. 2. Cherokee women—Biography—Juvenile literature. 3. Cherokee Indians—Kings and rulers—Juvenile literature. 4. Cherokee Indians—Politics and government—Juvenile literature. I. Title. II. Series.
   E99.C5M3345 1994
   973'.04975'092—dc20
   [B]   94-1229

Summary: A biography of Wilma Mankiller, the first woman to be elected chief of the Cherokee Nation.

Dillon Press
Macmillan Publishing Company
866 Third avenue
New York, Ny 10022

Maxwell Macmillan Canada, Inc.
1200 Eglinton Avenue East
Suite 200
Don Mills, Ontario M3C 3N1

Macmillan Publishing Company is part of the Maxwell Communication Group of Companies.

First Edition

Printed in the United States of America

10 9 8 7 6 5 4 3 21

Contents

There are so many forces working against Indian tribes. There are people . . . who don't realize our communities exist as they do today, that we have a language that is alive, that we have a tribal government that is thriving.

—Wilma Mankiller

Introduction

Even the most open-minded people might wonder how a person named Mankiller could attract enough voters to be elected chief of the Cherokee Nation—the largest Indian tribe in the United States after the Navajo. Still others wonder how a woman, regardless of her threatening name, could win the highest post in an Indian tribe governed for centuries by men. But on December 15, 1985, after Cherokee chief Ross Swimmer resigned from office, his deputy, Wilma Mankiller, was sworn in as the first female chief in Cherokee history. And two years later, with the support of both male and female voters, she was elected to her first full term as principal chief—not in spite of her name, but maybe in small part because of it.

In the 18th century the name Mankiller referred to a top military rank adopted by one of Wilma's warrior ancestors. The name is highly respected among tribe members and is a name to be proud of. Even after she married, she used her maiden name as her surname. But it was her work as a peaceful warrior fighting for Indian rights and self-sufficiency

Principal Chief Wilma P. Mankiller as she prepares to address the Cherokee Nation tribal council

that won the hearts—and the votes—of her people.

Most of the Cherokee Nation (130,000 members to date) had lived in poverty for generations. "Given half a chance," Chief Mankiller once said, the Cherokees "had tremendous potential to solve their own problems." And she told the *Chicago Tribune* that she hoped to be remembered "as the person who helped us restore faith in ourselves." She knew about poverty and lack of equal opportunity first-hand, from her own experience growing up on a farm in Oklahoma. Like most American Indians, her family could only dream about having electricity and indoor plumbing—luxuries that only white people enjoyed.

During the late 1960s Wilma Mankiller became active in the American Indian Rights movement and raised funds to support public protests against the unfair treatment of American Indians. Later, she formed the Community Development Department of the Cherokee Nation in Oklahoma (home of the tribe), and her many self-help projects have won national acclaim.

Chief Mankiller at a ceremony in her honor in Tahlequah, Oklahoma

Her work to integrate the best of both worlds—Indian and non-Indian—comes naturally to Wilma, because her mother is Caucasian and her father was a full-blooded Cherokee. As she told *Ms. Magazine*, "We have kept the best of our old ways of life and incorporated the sounder elements of today's non-Indian world." And the many awards she has received are encouraging, she believes, if only because the accompanying publicity helps to enlighten the rest of the country about the Cherokees. Yet it is her personal story of overcoming hardships—including a rare form of muscular dystrophy, kidney disease, and a near-fatal automobile accident—that makes her commitment to her tribe especially laudable.

To the Cherokees and other American Indians, Wilma Mankiller is both a role model and a symbol—a symbol of their own ability to triumph over adversity, "given half a chance."

Before Columbus

It would be useless to write about my life without including history.

—Wilma Mankiller

Centuries before Christopher Columbus was born, the Cherokee tribe was thriving in America—in areas later known as Georgia, Tennessee, Virginia, North Carolina, South Carolina, Kentucky, and Alabama. Its rich culture, in existence long before European contact, is envied by environmentalists today. Committed to the protection of the earth, the Cherokee culture was founded on a respect for nature and pursuit of harmony among all living things. This native culture, as described in *Cherokee Nation Communications*, sharply contrasted with the white European philosophy that was "directed toward conquering and controlling nature and the environment . . . cited often [today] as the cause of pollution and destruction."

After 1540, when the Cherokees discovered Spanish explorer Hernando de Soto and other white men in their homeland, tribe members began

◀ Chief Mankiller in the office of the council chamber of the Cherokee Nation

to exchange parts of their land for goods offered by the white settlers. In 1775 the Cherokees traded parts of Kentucky and Tennessee for guns and ammunition to protect themselves. It was the largest territory surrendered in frontier history. And in 1777 the Cherokees relinquished over five million acres of land. More treaties with the United States government—and more loss of Cherokee land—followed. Some treaties provided help "to assist the Indian in adapting to white civilization." Though the U.S. Supreme Court recognized Cherokee tribal sovereignty in Georgia, President Andrew Jackson ignored the ruling, thus paving the way for the historic New Echota Treaty.

By 1835 there was little left of the Cherokee Nation. In that year the New Echota Treaty was signed by a few dissident Cherokees, giving up all remaining territory east of the Mississippi River in exchange for land called Indian Territory (now Oklahoma). They also received "the promise of money, cattle, and other goods." And the Cherokees all had to move to the new Indian territory, as ordered by the United States government.

"When the Cherokee leaders signed that treaty," Cherokee Nation Communications reported, "they also signed their death warrants." Chief John Ross and the majority of Cherokees hoped to keep their tribal land and strongly opposed the New Echota Treaty, which mandated forced removal of the Cherokees. But President Jackson and the state of Georgia—where gold had been discovered—were victorious. Jackson ordered the United States Army to enforce the Removal Act, and, beginning in 1838, 17,000 Cherokees were sent from their homeland in the southeastern United States across the Mississippi to Indian Territory. They walked more than 1,000 miles—across Tennessee, Kentucky, Illinois, Missouri, and Arkansas. Approximately 3,000 died of starvation and disease during the long, painful march, which became known as the Trail of Tears. Another thousand fled to the Great Smoky Mountains.

In Indian Territory the survivors of the Trail of Tears established their own government, schools,

An artist's portrayal of the march that became known as the Trail of Tears

businesses, and bilingual newspapers. And even before Oklahoma became a state (in 1907), the Cherokees had reached a higher level of literacy than all the white communities around! But in the 60 years that followed, the decline of Cherokee achievement was dramatic. In *National Forum* Chief Mankiller recalled that sad period:

> The Cherokee people went from being literate to having one of the lowest levels of educational attainment in Oklahoma. The best

16

Chief Mankiller watches some Cherokee Nation Head Start students work on the computer.

argument possible for the support of tribal government begins with a comparison of where our people were when we had some real control over our own destiny and what happened to us when there was a strong attempt to abolish our government.

Chief Mankiller is naturally proud of the perseverance of her ancestors, and wants to stay on the same path as her immediate predecessors, who have worked hard to restore the vitality of the Cherokee Nation. Already she has shown the world how one woman can transcend the most debilitating barriers and become leader of an Indian nation within a non-Indian world. While encouraging harmony, she never forgets her own past and the importance of keeping the Cherokee tribal language and culture alive.

A Family on the Move

Wilma Pearl Mankiller was born on November 18, 1945, in Tahlequah, Oklahoma. She spent her early childhood on the family farm in a community called Mankiller Flats. Her grandfather had received the land from the United States government in its settlement with the Cherokees at the turn of the century. At that time, Cherokee land was allotted to individual families in an effort to break up tribal land holdings.

All of Irene and Charley Mankiller's children helped out on the farm, where they lived without any electricity, plumbing, telephone, or television. Though the children had horses to ride, they rode them mainly for a practical purpose—to get water from nearby springs. (Without indoor plumbing, daily trips to the springs were mandatory.) Wilma's family was poor, but they had fun together picking strawberries, green beans, and other crops produced on the farm.

Wilma and her brothers and sisters loved to play games together, too, and to join their parents and friends in community festivals, including cere-

Wilma (middle row on right) and her brothers and sisters at Mankiller Flats in Oklahoma

monial dances in the moonlight. At home, the family would gather around the battery-operated radio for special programs they could all enjoy. To Wilma, the family gatherings were cherished times; it was the shared fun she always remembered—not the programs themselves.

Most of all, Wilma liked to read (the house was filled with books) and to listen to tales of Indian lore passed on from generation to generation by her relatives. Years later, in her autobiography, *Mankiller: A Chief and Her People*, she herself would pass on some favorite Cherokee stories, including this tale about the origin of the earth:

> In the beginning, before Mother Earth was made, there was only a vast body of water that was both salty and fresh. There were no human beings, only animals. They lived in the heavens above the sea. They were secure in a solid rock sky vault called Galunlati. As the animals, birds, and insects multiplied, the sky became more crowded

and there was a fear that some creatures would be pushed off the sky rock. All the creatures called a council to decide what to do. At last . . . the little Water-beetle, called Dayunsi, offered to leave the sky and investigate the water below. Water-beetle darted in every direction over the water's surface, but could not find any place to rest. So the beetle dived to the bottom of the sea and returned with soft mud, which began to grow and spread until it became known as earth.

As a young girl, Wilma was not aware of the sense of values she was learning from her parents. It never dawned on her that her responsibilities on the farm and in the community would prepare her for the highest post in the Cherokee Nation. Years later she told *National Forum* the importance of community spirit to the Cherokee:

In many native communities there is much greater emphasis on the collective achievements of the family or the community than those of the individual. Native people who have achieved great personal success, though respected, are not held in the same esteem as those who have achieved great success in helping others. The latter are held in the highest esteem.

Growing up close to the land gave Wilma a deep respect for the earth. Growing up in poverty taught her empathy for other Indians in America. Though she was small in size, soft-spoken and thoughtful, Wilma was developing great inner strength to meet the many challenges ahead.

Bloom Where You Are Planted

After a long drought, the farm could no longer support the Mankiller family, and they had to leave Oklahoma. In 1957 the Bureau of Indian Affairs moved them and other Indian families to San Francisco, California, as part of the "mainstreaming" process. According to the bureau, placing Indians in the mainstream of America was a positive move to help Indians adjust to city life. But for the Mankillers, moving from the farm to San Francisco was like rocketing to the moon. And they missed the peace and quiet of the country much more. Wilma missed her friends and the whole Cherokee community. Years later she explained that disruptive time in her life to *Ms.* Magazine:

Relocation was yet another answer from the federal government to the continuing dilemma of what to do with us. We are a people with many, many social indicators of decline and an awful lot of problems, so in the fifties they decided to mainstream us, to try to take us away from the tribal land base and

the tribal culture, [and] get us into the cities.
It was supposed to be a better life.

Wilma had never seen a tall building before she moved to San Francisco. She had never been in an elevator, and had only dreamed about riding a bicycle and using a telephone. She wondered if she would ever get used to her new life in the city—where the lights at night were so dazzling that she no longer noticed the moon. Later she told a reporter about the culture shock she experienced: "One day I was there [on the farm] and the next day I was trying to deal with the mysteries of television, indoor plumbing, neon lights, and elevators."

Riding bicycles and talking on the phone couldn't make up for the loneliness that 12-year-old Wilma felt during the first months in California. Her family lived in a poor section of San Francisco— a ghetto—and were the only Cherokees there. They felt like foreigners, completely uprooted and alone. But the Mankillers seemed to live by an old adage, "Bloom where you are planted," because that is exactly what they did.

Wilma's father found a job in a warehouse and soon afterward became a union activist. He was "the only full-blooded Indian union organizer I ever ran into," Wilma told an interviewer.

The Mankiller children went to public schools, but as times grew tougher, the oldest son had to leave school to help support the family.

Following high school Wilma studied sociology at San Francisco State University. During that time she met an accountant from Ecuador, whom she later married. In 1964 Wilma's first daughter, Felicia, was born, followed by the birth of another daughter, Gina, two years later.

The early 1960's was a time when young people began to protest the lack of equal opportunity for minorities, and Wilma echoed their outcry in her own way. Distressed by the growing poverty Indians were suffering under United States government control, Wilma seized the opportunity to stand up for what she believed in. In 1969 young American Indians organized the America Indian Rights move-

Wilma (right) and a friend attend a pow-wow in the San Francisco Bay area.

ment to bring attention to their plight. Wilma wanted to help them.

The protesters took over the empty Alcatraz prison in San Francisco, and Wilma raised funds for their cause. During the 18-month occupation of the prison, Wilma worked nonstop to keep their nonviolent protest alive. She later explained her reasons for her involvement to John Hughes of the *Chicago Tribune*: "Those college students who participated in Alcatraz articulated a lot of feelings I had that I'd never been able to express. I was a mother, so I couldn't join them, but I did fund raising and got involved in the activist movement."

Her work on behalf of the Alcatraz protest changed the whole course of her life. In addition to taking college classes at night, Wilma worked as the Native American Programs coordinator for the Oakland, California, public school system during the day. Her two daughters and her commitment to her work became her most important concerns. Her 10-year marriage ended, and in the mid-1970s she divorced her husband and, with Felicia and Gina, returned to the land she loved and missed so much—Mankiller Flats, where the family farm is, in Oklahoma. Above all, as she told John Hughes, "I wanted my children to experience the rural life . . . and I thought some of the skills I'd learned [in San Francisco] I could practice here."

Once again Wilma began to bloom where she was planted. She built a little wooden house on the family property, and as her parents had done in the past, she filled the shelves with books: the works of Plato, Chaucer, Tolstoy, and Kant. Her mother had already returned to the farm, and her brothers and sisters followed. Her father had died in 1971, but he was buried nearby. So the family was together again on the farm they all loved.

Wilma worked as economic-stimulus coordinator for the Cherokee nation. She also earned a B.A. in social science, and in 1979 did graduate study in community planning at the nearby University of Arkansas. "My goal has always been for Indians to solve their own problems," she told *Fortune* magazine. On the way to her goal, she raised funds to start the Community Development Department of the Cherokee Nation, and a few years later became its director.

The year 1979 was memorable for tragic events, too. While Wilma was driving home from the university, she crashed into another car, driven by a friend. Her friend died. Wilma suffered severe injuries that required 17 operations, including plastic surgery to reconstruct her face. At the same time she was told she had a rare form of muscular dystrophy. But after receiving chemotherapy, the disease went into remission. She told John Hughes, "In a way it seems it was a test of perseverance . . . that I went through. It was a maturing kind of process. It was a definite preparation."

In 1971 the Cherokee tribe in Oklahoma had begun to again elect its own government, which included a principal chief, a deputy chief, and a tribal council to make laws. When Principal Chief Ross Swimmer ran for reelection in 1983, he surprised some people by asking Wilma Mankiller to run as candidate for deputy chief. Her skills impressed

Chief Mankiller at work in her office

him. And her innovative community projects to help the Cherokees revive their self-esteem and quality of life had caught his attention during his first administration. Though his conservative, Republican background contrasted sharply with Mankiller's liberal, Democratic views, Chief Swimmer knew she was committed to the Cherokee Nation and to the "pursuit of happiness" for all American Indians. Besides, he said, "She is one sharp businesswoman!"

Wilma Mankiller had started programs that no one had ever tried before, and her skillful management impressed Indian and non-Indian leaders alike. Her Bell Community Project established 16 miles of water lines in Bell, Oklahoma, so that at last Indians could have running water in their homes. Her restoration of houses in Bell caught the whole nation's attention because of the scope of the project and her determination to see Indians live in dignity. And her ability to write and secure grants for community development, including everything from social programs to landscaping, made a lasting impression on Chief Swimmer. He was excited about having Wilma as his deputy chief.

In 1983 Swimmer and Mankiller won the election, and the press praised the new chief for selecting a woman as his running mate. Word spread quickly that for the first time in its history the Cherokee Nation had a female deputy chief. But the election was just a prelude to the most significant event in Mankiller's life—and in the life of her tribe.

Listening to Sequoyah

Two years after Ross Swimmer was reelected chief of the Cherokee Nation, President Ronald Reagan appointed him director of the Bureau of Indian Affairs in Washington, D.C. The deputy chief— Wilma Mankiller—then automatically moved into the highest post in the tribe.

On December 15, 1985, she took the oath of office. "Memories of my public inauguration will stay with me as long as I live," she later wrote in her autobiography. "Many people felt that the Cherokee Nation would crash and burn with a woman in charge. I was very wary. I knew full well what was ahead."

The media swarmed around her to cover the historic event. "How does it feel to be the first female chief of your tribe?" "What do the men think of your new role?" Such questions were fired at Chief Mankiller repeatedly. Her response to Robert Reinhold of the New York Times summed up her feelings about the "woman question." "The Cherokees," she told him, "are more worried about jobs and education, not whether the tribe is run by a woman or not."

◄ *Chief Mankiller at her 1987 inauguration as Principal Chief of the Cherokee Nation*

In fact, it was only after the North American Indian tribes came into contact with white people that a "male-oriented system of government" was followed by the Indians, Mankiller said. Originally, the tribes were matrilineal, with women playing significant roles in the tribe. Chief Mankiller explains that her role as chief is not as revolutionary as it seems:

Early historians referred to our government as a petticoat government because of the strong role of the women in the tribe. Then, we adopted a lot of ugly things that were part of the non-Indian world, and one of those things was sexism. . . . So, in 1687 women enjoyed a prominent role, but in 1987 we found people questioning whether women should be in leadership positions anywhere in the tribe. So my election was a step forward and a step backward at the same time.

The election of 1987—the first time Wilma Mankiller ran for office on her own—proved her popularity among the Cherokees, both male and female. Her second husband, Charlie Soap, whom she had married the year before, helped her campaign, and his command of the Cherokee language was a great asset. Though it was a close election, she defeated her opponent, Perry Wheeler, 5,914 votes to 4,670. She promised her tribe members that she would focus on their 20 percent unemployment rate, their low level of literacy, and their great need for economic development. And she did.

One of her most important concerns was—and still is—the education of Cherokee children. She pledged to revive the tribal language and culture, and to fulfill that pledge she created the Institute for Cherokee Literacy. Students study there in the summer months, and, on return to their communities, they spread their knowledge of reading and writing the Cherokee language to others.

Learning the Cherokee alphabet would not only improve the literacy level, Mankiller believed, but also would lift community spirit. Her determination

Chief Mankiller talks with a 10-year-old Cherokee girl at a ceremony near Tahlequah.

to educate her people echoed that of "the Cherokee genius" Sequoyah. It was Sequoyah who had developed the Cherokee alphabet in the 18th century. It was his love of teaching and communicating with others that led to the publication of the *Cherokee*

Cherokee Alphabet.

Ꭰ a	Ꭱ e	Ꭲ i	Ꭳ o	Ꭴ u	Ꭵ v
Ꭶ ga Ꭷ ka	Ꭸ ge	Ꭹ gi	Ꭺ go	Ꭻ gu	Ꭼ gv
Ꭽ ha	Ꭾ he	Ꭿ hi	Ꮀ ho	Ꮁ hu	Ꮂ hv
Ꮃ la	Ꮄ le	Ꮅ li	Ꮆ lo	Ꮇ lu	Ꮈ lv
Ꮉ ma	Ꮊ me	Ꮋ mi	Ꮌ mo	Ꮍ mu	
Ꮎ na Ꮏ hna Ꮐ nah	Ꮑ ne	Ꮒ ni	Ꮓ no	Ꮔ nu	Ꮕ nv
Ꮖ qua	Ꮗ que	Ꮘ qui	Ꮙ quo	Ꮚ quu	Ꮛ quv
Ꮜ sa Ꮝ s	Ꮞ se	Ꮟ si	Ꮠ so	Ꮡ su	Ꮢ sv
Ꮣ da Ꮤ ta	Ꮥ de Ꮦ te	Ꮧ di Ꮨ ti	Ꮩ do	Ꮪ du	Ꮫ dv
Ꮬ dla Ꮭ tla	Ꮮ tle	Ꮯ tli	Ꮰ tlo	Ꮱ tlu	Ꮲ tlv
Ꮳ tsa	Ꮴ tse	Ꮵ tsi	Ꮶ tso	Ꮷ tsu	Ꮸ tsv
Ꮹ wa	Ꮺ we	Ꮻ wi	Ꮼ wo	Ꮽ wu	Ꮾ wv
Ꮿ ya	Ᏸ ye	Ᏹ yi	Ᏺ yo	Ᏻ yu	Ᏼ yv

Sounds Represented by Vowels

a, as a in father, or short as a in rival
e, as a in hate, or short as e in met
i, as i in pique, or short as i in pit
o, as o in note, approaching aw in law
u, as oo in fool, or short as u in pull
v, as u in but, nasalized

Consonant Sounds

g nearly as in English, but approaching to k. d nearly as in English but approaching to t. h k l m n q s t w y as in English. Syllables beginning with g except Ꭶ (ga) have sometimes the power of k. Ꭺ (go), Ꮪ (du), Ꮫ (dv) are sometimes sounded to, tu, tv and syllables written with tl except Ꮭ (tla) sometimes vary to dl.

Chief Mankiller enjoying the company of some Cherokee Nation Head Start students

Phoenix, the first Indian newspaper published in North America. When Sequoyah was a young boy he watched white people read books, and he called the pages "talking leaves." Later, he spent 12 years forming the Cherokee alphabet, completing it in 1821. In just six months the Cherokees who spoke the language could read it. The *Cherokee Phoenix* was first published in 1828, in both English and Cherokee. Sequoyah could neither read nor write English; more important to him was communication among the Cherokees in their own language. "Monuments to him soar as high as the giant Sequoia Redwood trees of California, which were named in his honor," *Cherokee Nation Communications* reports.

The *Cherokee Phoenix* has been revived under a new name, the *Cherokee Advocate*, and it is read by more tribe members today than ever before. And if Chief Mankiller has her way, Sequoyah's legacy will stay alive forever.

The Torch Is Passed

As a team, Wilma Mankiller and Ross Swimmer had taken giant steps toward their goal of Cherokee independence. New businesses opened, ranging from a motel to a poultry ranch. And a new harmony developed between full-blooded and mixed-blooded Cherokees. When the torch was passed to Chief Mankiller, she promised to "stay in the same path" forged by Chief Swimmer and herself.

One project close to Mankiller's heart is the building of a hydroelectric plant, which would provide many jobs for tribe members as well as make innovative use of tribal lands. "I'd like to see whole, healthy communities again," she told *Ms.* Magazine, "communities in which tribe members would have access to adequate health care, higher education if they want it, a decent place to live, a decent place to work, and a strong commitment to tribal language and culture."

Chief Mankiller brought all of the new businesses and land development under the newly created Department of Commerce. And gift shops have been added to the long list of emerging enter-

◄ *Chief Mankiller visits one of the Cherokee-run businesses that she has helped to get started.*

prises she has fostered. "One of the biggest problems," she told the *New York Times*, "is that we need to really trust our own selves and our own thinking, and not allow others to convince us that our thoughts, ideas, plans, and visions aren't valid." Though she is "small and stocky," as the *Current Biography Yearbook* describes her, Wilma Mankiller has become a powerful figure in American Indians' nonviolent struggles for self-esteem and for independence from the United States government.

In 1990, for example, she signed the historic self-governance agreement, which gave the Cherokee Nation and five other tribes the opportunity to manage $6.1 million in funds previously directed by the Bureau of Indian Affairs and its branch offices. The agreement was a major leap for the Cherokee tribe—and for its chief, who had dreamed about self-rule for Indians ever since she was a teenager. *Cherokee Nation Communications* reported the significance of the new legislation:

The agreement authorizes the tribe to plan,

President Ronald Reagan meets with Chief Mankiller and other American Indian leaders at the White House.

In her office in Tahlequah, Chief Mankiller holds a poster given to her by a local artist.

46

conduct, consolidate and administer programs and receive direct funding to deliver services to tribal members. Self-governance is a change from the paternalistic controls the federal government has exercised in the past to full tribal responsibility for self-government and independence intended by the treaties with sovereign Indian nations. . . . Tribal governmental officials and citizens will determine where appropriations can be best spent for their needs, and they will be responsible and accountable for the federal assets and annual appropriations which will be transferred directly and totally to the tribal government for the service of citizens who will elect those officials through a constitutional government. Moreover, funding for law enforcement will give tribes the authority to ensure accountability of elected or employed tribal officials.

Also under Wilma Mankiller's leadership, a new

tax code was approved—including tobacco and sales taxes—to provide governmental services and economic development for the Cherokees. In addition, a court system and legal code was established, adding still more self-sufficiency for the Cherokee Nation. After the code was enacted in 1990, four more legal acts provided a Penal Code, a Uniform Vehicle Code, and a Uniform Controlled Dangerous Substance Act.

Since Mankiller was first elected chief in 1987, the Cherokee Nation Industries has grown steadily; more than two-thirds of the Cherokees have been employed, and have earned approximately $3.5 million in the industries' Stilwell community headquarters. Its success is marked, too, by the annual $500,000 it turns over the the Cherokee Nation. Also, as in other American Indian tribes, bingo outposts have added income for the Nation. But Chief Mankiller encourages more enriching, more long-lasting enterprises for tribal members. "I really don't think Bingo will provide a stable economy for our tribe," she told the *New York Times*. "I would rather do things that would last a long time."

Wilma Mankiller is especially proud that the Cherokee Nation in Oklahoma is "on the map" for its leadership role in education, health care, housing, economic development, and vocational training. The Talking Leaves Job Corps, for example, offers young people the preparation they need for the many jobs that continue to emerge as the Cherokees develop their 7,000-square-mile area.

Woman of the Year

In 1986 the Oklahoma Federation of Indian Women named Wilma Mankiller Woman of the Year, and in 1987 she received the same honor from *Ms.* Magazine in New York. Also in 1987, Mankiller was elected to the board of the *Ms.* Foundation for Women. "I think I represent a different kind of Cherokee feminism," she told *Ms.* reporter Michele Wallace. "What I consider to be women's work—by that I mean work that promotes the role of women in society—is done within the context of the community. I have a strong feeling that if I bring women and men together, that is just as much a part of my role as to educate sexist men."

She received an honorary doctorate from the University of New England in Maine, and in 1986 the Harvard Foundation honored her with its Distinguished Service Citation. Her long list of awards also includes an honorary doctorate of humane letters from Yale University, and, in 1991, an honorary doctorate from Dartmouth College. That same year she was reelected principal chief of the Cherokee Nation—this time with more than 80 percent of the vote.

◄ *Wilma Mankiller, who feels she represents a different kind of Cherokee feminism, has been honored by various women's groups.*

For Wilma Mankiller, the greatest rewards in her role as chief of the Cherokee Nation come from the achievements of her people—from the education of the children, the self-sufficiency of the elderly, and from the rebuilding of the Nation's self-esteem. More than anything, she wants to erase the negative stereotypes of Indians that permeate the non-Indian world. In "Education and Native Americans," published in *National Forum*, she explains why Americans know so little about Native people:

> There is a woeful absence of accurate information, either historical or contemporary, about Native people. Most people fill this void with negative stereotypes from old Westerns [movies] or romanticized paintings and collections in museums. My friend, a Seneca scholar, once remarked that many people have a mental snapshot of Native people taken three hundred years ago and want to retain that image. It is with this backdrop that Native students enter college.

Chief Mankiller hopes to erase the negative stereotypes of Indians that often exist in the non-Indian world.

The farther one goes from a tribal land base to attend college, the more stereotypes Native students must deal with. . . . In the past few years academia has become more and more aware of the fact that the minority population is increasing, while the corresponding numbers of minority students enrolling in institutions of higher education have declined.

It is the decline of minority students in colleges that deeply concerns Chief Mankiller, her colleagues, and educators. "All Americans should be concerned," she says, and they should ask themselves this question: "From what sources will business, industry, and government draw their workforce in a decade or two?" The labor pool will consist of minority people, "many of whom have not had an opportunity for a solid higher education," she says.

Students who are raised in traditional tribal families look at education in a different way than non-

Indian students do. In tribal families, Mankiller explains, "the value of a formal education is not measured by personal, or economic goals." Native students see their education at school as a part of their total education, which includes spirituality and moral codes learned at home and in the community. "Spirituality," Mankiller writes, "is not just something one expresses once a week by dressing up and attending Sunday-morning services. Rather, spiritual values are incorporated into all aspects of daily life. . . . Education in some tribal communities need not take place only while one sits in a classroom memorizing specific facts."

Chief Mankiller is especially proud of the sense of interdependence that is deeply rooted in Native Americans. As she has said many times, it is the collective achievements of the family or community that Cherokees value so highly, rather than individual acts. It is team spirit in the truest sense: The players form the team, and the team is the star. The same spirit guides Cherokee family life. "Grandparents and extended family members either live in [the same] households or live close by," Chief Mankiller writes. "Family members pass on stories that may have a . . . simple plot, but there is always a value or moral to be learned from the story [that adds to the total education of the children]. Education is an ongoing lifetime process that exists not in a vacuum but as a part of the whole."

Years ago Wilma Mankiller believed that preparation for college or other higher education should begin in junior high school. But today she says, "I believe that preparation for higher education probably begins with good prenatal care." Such care is provided by the Women, Infants, and Children Program, a Cherokee support service that "has probably contributed more than we will ever know to higher education." And she is pleased that after 20 years of educational programs—including adult literacy courses, Head Start after-school programs, student and family counseling services, financial aid, and scholarships—the Cherokee people have reached new levels of achievement in the field of education. But, she says, more support is needed

Wilma with husband Charlie Soap and Charlie's son ▶

for all of the programs designed to educate Cherokee young people. "We cannot . . . undertake this task alone," she asserts.

To better understand the goals of the Cherokee Nation today, one must recall the history of the tribe, Chief Mankiller believes. Knowing about the struggles the Cherokees faced and about their golden age, which came and went so tragically, we can understand—and welcome—the renewed vitality of the tribe.

In "Education and Native Americans," she summarizes some of that history:

> After the Trail of Tears, the Cherokee people pulled themselves together despite the great loss of lives and homes, and the political and social upheaval. They began the task of building a new government in Indian Territory. They built beautiful government structures that still stand today as the oldest buildings in Oklahoma; they started a newspaper, which was published in Cherokee and

English; and most important, they built an educational system for tribal members. The Cherokee Seminaries were among the first educational systems built west of the Mississippi—Indian or non-Indian. In fact . . . during the mid-19th century the Cherokee population was more literate than the neighboring non-Indian population.

She explains that after Oklahoma became a state and the Cherokees came under United States control, the tribe declined, their government "went into disarray," and their schools closed. But their community spirit and brilliant leadership have once again triumphed, and the Cherokee Nation has won worldwide praise for its many accomplishments.

Chief Mankiller refuses to accept all the credit for her tribe's success under her leadership. She insists that she could not have succeeded without the continued support of her tribal employees, the tribal council, and her deputy chief. They are a team. Together they govern the 130,000 tribal

Chief Mankiller stands by a flag bearing the seal of the Cherokee Nation.

members and manage an annual budget of more than $66 million.

Standing in her office, beneath the Cherokee Nation seal on the wall behind her, Chief Wilma Mankiller points out that the words SEAL OF THE CHEROKEE NATION appear in both English and Cherokee. The Native characters are from the alphabet created by Sequoyah, "the Cherokee genius" and beloved ancestor of the tribe members. But today it is their chief—the first female chief in Cherokee history—who symbolizes the creative genius of their tribe.

For Further Reading

Glassman, Bruce. *Wilma Mankiller: Chief of the Cherokee Nation.* New York: Blackbirch Press/Rosen, 1992.

Green, Rayna, ed. *Women in American Indian Society.* New York: Chelsea House, 1992.

Mails, Thomas E. *The Cherokee People.* Tulsa: Council Oak Books, 1992.

Mankiller, Wilma, and Michael Wallis. *Mankiller: A Chief and Her People.* New York: St. Martin's Press, 1993.

Perdue, Theda. *The Cherokee.* New York: Chelsea House, 1989.

Waldman, Carl. *Atlas of the North American Indian.* New York: Facts on File, 1985.

Index

About the Author

Caroline Evensen Lazo was born in Minneapolis, Minnesota. She spent much of her childhood visiting museums and attending plays written by her mother, Isobel Evensen, whose work earned national acclaim and became a lasting source of inspiration for her daughter.

Ms. Lazo attended the University of Oslo, Norway, and received a B.A. in Art History from the University of Minnesota. She has written extensively about art and architecture, and is the author of many books for young people, including *The Terra Cotta Army of Emperor Qin, Missing Treasure,* and *Endangered Species.*